To my dear friend
Dr. Jim Wagner
—L.R.R.

To Henry
—B.H.

BEAR'S BIG BREAKFAST

By
Lynn Rowe Reed

Illustrated by
Brett Helquist

BALZER + BRAY
An Imprint of HarperCollins*Publishers*

I'm starved.
I feel like breakfast.

Hello there, **Bunny**.
I am famished.

What are you in the
mood for?

I'll help you find
a yummier breakfast.

Good morning, Bumblebee.
Do you taste good?

Of course! I am delicious. But
let me give you a kiss before you
eat me up.

I've changed my mind.

Then I will help you find breakfast.

Hola, Boa!
We come in peace.
I am looking for something
to eat, like maybe a
b-b-b-b-b—
I forget.

Here, try this bark.

Bark is not tasty!

Then we will
find you something
with more flavor.

I am hungrier than
ever. I am so hungry
I could eat a **bat**!

Wait! I am too bony for bears!
I will help you find a better breakfast.

Howdy, **Bluebird**!
Will you be my breakfast?

I would, Bear, but who will
take care of my beautiful babies?
I'll help you look for breakfast!

I am *so-o-o-o-o* sleepy.

I think . . . I need . . .

a nap.

Balzer + Bray is an imprint of HarperCollins Publishers.

Bear's Big Breakfast

Text copyright © 2016 by Lynn Rowe Reed. Illustrations copyright © 2016 by Brett Helquist.

ISBN 978-0-06-226455-8

The artist used acrylic and oil paints to create the illustrations for this book.

Typography by Dana Fritts

16 17 18 19 20   SCP   10 9 8 7 6 5 4 3 2 1

❖

First Edition